The Little Bu

MW00897656

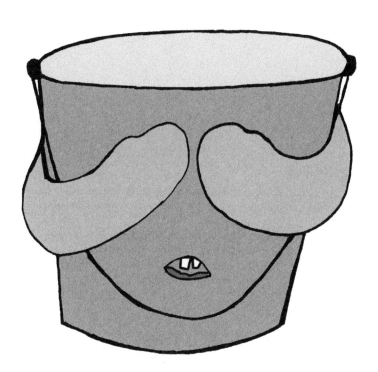

Jeffrey Bates

For Harrison, Bayleigh and Joseph

© 2014 Jeffrey Bates
All Rights Reserved.

No part of this publication may be reproduced, stored in a retrieval system, or transmitted, in any form or by any means, electronic, mechanical, photocopying, recording, or otherwise, without the written permission of the author.

First published by Dog Ear Publishing
4010 W. 86th Street, Ste H
Indianapolis, IN 46268
www.dogearpublishing.net

ISBN: 978-1-4575-2751-7

This book is printed on acid-free paper.

This book is a work of fiction. Places, events, and situations in this book are purely fictional and any resemblance to actual persons, living or dead, is coincidental.

Printed in the United States of America

Foreword

A myth carries a truth that touches us at a soul level. A myth teaches us about deeper truths in a way that sparks our imagination. A myth is a story that is more real than real. Jeff Bates has written a poetic story that contains many elements of myth. He has written of real psychological and spiritual truths that go down with the sugar of story. That is the hallmark of a myth.

Myths draw us into a story that speaks to the child in us as well as to the children of this world. A child often understands the message of a myth better than many adults. The child feels the story. I think Jeff's intent is for children to not only feel the story, but to try and live it. In seeing the world through the eyes of the Bucket, children can learn the lessons of compassion tempered with self-love. However, the lesson that may be this book's most important mythic message is that happiness is an *inside* job.

Symbols are the language of myth. Myths teach us in symbols. The more we work with symbols the more meaning can unfold, because symbols reveal an inner mystery. Children don't question mystery. They are drawn to live it. That is why it is so important to be careful with the stories we tell them. Jeff has been very careful to give us all a story that we can see, understand and live well.

Larry Pesavento
Psychotherapist and Director of the Christos Center in Cincinnati, Ohio
January 2014

Acknowledgements

One day, as I was talking to my 12 year old son about his responsibilities for picking up his socks and not leaving them laying the middle of the living room floor, again, I noted to him that telling him things like this sometimes felt like I was pouring water into a bucket with a hole in the bottom. What I put in doesn't stay, and it just runs right through. It was in this context that the Little Bucket woke up inside of me. I didn't know if other parents could relate, nor did I know if anyone else had ever thought of this metaphor, but it didn't matter, because my words, the words of this poem, began to flow to me and I sat down and poured them out onto a piece of paper. I played and splashed and was thrilled with the twists and flow of the words and phrases as I wrote. It seemed that I was floating down a river. I had no way of predicting where the river would take me, but when the trip was over, the view took me to a realization that I wanted to share. The illustrations also began to appear in my head, like a daydream, and soon I began sketching them. What you hold in your hands is that realization. Though this is a children's book, I believe that anyone who reads it and feels it will experience something for which there may be no words. There is a child down deep in all of us. And children can teach us things.

I thank my friend and mentor Larry Pesavento for writing the Foreword. We have had a wonderful time talking about myth and stories over the last 20 years. I will be forever grateful for his friendship. I also thank those who read the book, my friends Larry Burnley, Teresa Hatten, Richard Hamm and Michael Fallahay, and gave me feedback. I am grateful for those who read the book, including Larry Pesavento, and wrote the short reviews for the back cover: Mary Henderson, Richard Hamm, Philip Gulley and Roxanne Pace.

I dedicate this book to my wife, Becky, who is the most amazing person I have ever known and is a very full bucket! It's also dedicated to my two children, Harrison and Bayleigh. My hope is that they will grow up to be full, happy buckets. This short and mythical tale is also dedicated to another one of my teachers, who has helped me see the importance of understanding the place of myth and story in our lives, Joseph Campbell. If this book gets you interested in myth, Joseph Campbell is your go to for more about the power of myth and how we are all shaped and formed by the stories we've been given and by those we tell.

Jeffrey Bates
May 2014

The Little Bucket

There was once a little bucket

Who lived west of Nantucket

Where the sun was bright and shining

And the flowers were beautiful and reclining...

The cloud felt just the same.

Even the tree wanted to know his name.

He splished some here and he splashed some there.

No matter how much he splashed he had plenty to spare.

Splashing this much, it seemed so rare,

He could have been a dunk tank at the fair!

5

He played with his friends every day, and sometimes at night.

The fun that they had, well, there was no end in sight.

They splashed each other, they were *diggin'* it too,

They turned the dirt into mud and played in the goo!

Every day of the week he loved to play ball,

Until he heard his mother's call.

He knew right then it was time to go,

But not until his good friendship to show.

He laughed and he giggled and gave a high five!

There's no doubt about it, he felt really alive!

But not everyone could splash like he,

As a matter of fact some buckets seemed quite empty...

With nothing to spare and nothing to share.

So all he could do was offer his care.

So without a second thought, he jumped up in the air,

To show this friend that he really did care!

He poured and he splashed, there was no doubt,

That he gave and he gave until he almost ran out!

Later that day, as he walked home from school,

There was a trail behind him, it looked like some drool.

Some kids saw it, and were making fun,

And so the taunting had begun.

It wasn't nice, they were being mean,

Because of this line they had seen,

Running from his bucket and straight to the ground,

Which even caught the nose of a hound.

When he got home from school he was telling his mom

Of the many things that had gone on.

When she didn't listen, he went outside,

And attempted to hide from this feeling inside.

After all of this he felt something had changed

And that something inside of him felt rearranged.

He didn't know what it was, but his fullness had grown smaller.

He had given so much to that bucket who was taller.

Though the bucket wasn't empty, it had surely gone down.

And now he felt his face had a frown.

He tried and he tried to get filled back up,

He was a bucket, but he couldn't hold a cup!

Not a spigot, not a pond, nor raindrops from the sky,

There just wasn't enough to fill up this guy.

No matter how much went in, he still ran dry.

SPIGOT   POND   RAINDROPS

Buckets came from far and near to lend him help and aid.

These fine buckets called themselves "The Awesome Bucket Brigade."

Little ones, big ones, tall ones, short ones, young ones, old ones

And different colors too!

But what they put in, well, it just ran right through,

And it flowed all the way from here to Timbuktu.

No one knew why he felt so sad,

And they even made fun of the trouble he had.

They just didn't have any more words to say,

As they shrugged their shoulders and walked away.

He'd never felt this lonely or forgotten,

And didn't know why this trouble he had got in.

Some days passed and then he heard,

A voice that said, as softly as a bird,

"Look inside your bucket!"

But he thought "How?"

He was afraid he might find a *cow*!

When he looked inside, he found a hole,

Right there smack in the bottom of his soul!

A hole, a hole, it didn't seem right,

But he saw it there in plain sight!

A hole was there, it was nice and round,

And this hole it led right straight to the ground!

But around the hole, and I mean all around,

The universe, the stars and the galaxies did abound!

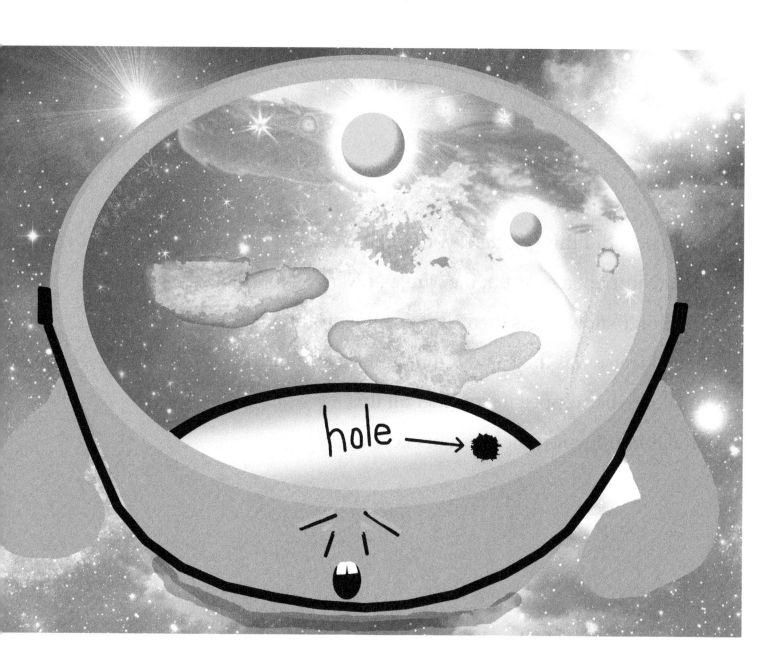

Well, how did this get there, you may have heard him squeal!

There's just not a hole, but the whole universe! Now that's a big deal!

He didn't know it was there, it was quite profound,

The universe was there and it didn't make a sound.

In silence he stopped to consider all this,

Not alone anymore, he was a bucket of bliss!

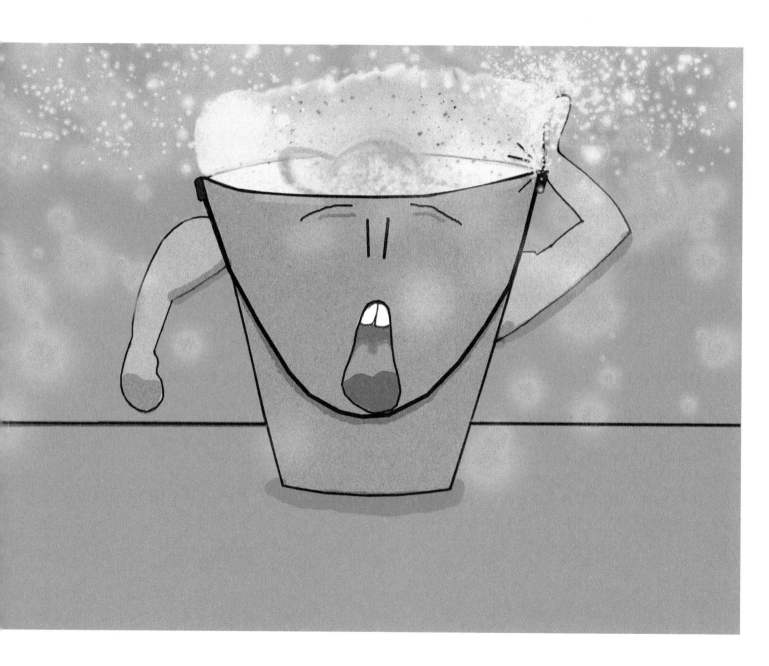

You just never know what will happen when you give yourself to another,

To a friend, a sister, mother or dad or a stinky little brother.

When you give your best, and give it some time, this truth often rings clear,

Sometimes what comes back to you can make your life more dear.

Even though for a time it caused some trouble or some pain,

What comes back into your bucket does more to plug the drain.

The message of the bucket comes as a gift and surprise to you and me,

In it we find a secret meant for *all* to see.

We can't really fill each other up like we would envision,

It seems that it's for every person, and that finding one self's the mission.

Now most of us are like the bucket, each child, each woman and man.

We live each day trying our best, doing all we can.

And something happens along the way to stir us from our sleep.

Its message is clear, if we can hear, it comes from somewhere deep.

Look inside, be a friend! Be a friend to yourself indeed!

It comes as a gift, with galaxies and stars, and will be there whenever you need.

And now the Bucket has come back to himself, he can feel his fullness again.

He's glad for his family, and the love of all his friends.

He splashes again, each moment is new, gleaming stars all around.

He's glad for this new place inside, and the wondrous universe he's found.

The End ~ *And The Beginning*

The Little Bucket - Some Reflections

I hope you have enjoyed reading and seeing this book. That Little Bucket didn't give up did he? He started off full, lost it all and then found the entire universe inside. It wasn't easy getting there and there was a lot of learning along the way, but he was determined to be filled up. Because he felt his emptiness, though at first he tried to hide from it, he was able to connect to the source and the wonder of who he is. Sometimes we have to go through a time of being empty before we can be full. It's just the way it seems to be. When we feel empty, we try to fill ourselves up with all kinds of things, and others try to fill us, but really nothing can and no one can fill us (i.e., make us happy) but ourselves. We, like The Little Bucket, have to find our FULL-fillment on the inside. That's where the good stuff is. If we wait for others to fill us, we are walking a path to be disappointed. This doesn't mean that we shouldn't be kind or considerate of others, but we have to ultimately realize that we can't make others happy, nor can they make us happy. We all have to learn that happiness comes from within. The whole world is deeply confused about this subject.

This book encourages children to be empathic. Empathy is the capacity to put oneself in someone else's shoes, or in this case, "bucket," and to imagine what they're feeling. Empathy is a skill that can help others feel the feelings they are hiding from. And it helps the person who feels your empathy to feel less alone. This skill is especially needed by adults, parents, teachers, ministers and therapists. In considering all of the implications of empathy, I ran across a very pertinent quote from a very famous counselor, who himself was thinking inside the bucket. Rollo May speaks about the importance of empathy by saying that empathy causes influence. And it's not just any normal influence, but, as the ancients understood it, an empathy that has celestial significance. He says, "Influence is one of the results of empathy...The word has it's root in the primitive astrological idea that an "in-flowing" of ethereal fluid from the stars affected the actions of men (sic), which is the early mythological recognition of the fact that influence occurs in the deep levels of the unconscious."* When one feels that someone is really listening to them, there is the effect of empathy, or, as I like to say, the experience of connectedness. We can feel connected to something deep inside us, like star power. If we can practice empathy, the star-power of the universe will empower those who might otherwise feel lost and lonely. They will discover what's really inside of them.

This short book has a mythical message for children that will stay with them a long time. When, in an age gone by, stories like this were told, they were told for a reason and they had a purpose. Stories rooted the spirit of humanity to the earth. The old stories, like the Grimm's Fairy Tales, for generations, spoke to something within that could not be spoken to in any other way. These stories shaped and gave depth and meaning to life. We often think of myth as an "untruth" or as an "untrue story." That is a common modern misunderstanding of the definition of myth. We live in an age when we have LOST the connection to the mythic world of our ancestors. And we are in desperate need to recover it. But, today, we find other myths shaping our lives and giving us meaning. Some of them include acquiring the latest and greatest electronic device which we think will make us happy, or that professional sports and the millions we spend on it really means something to the universe. These are just some of our myths. They are taking us out into space, just without a guidance system onboard.

When The Little Bucket discovers why he is not full, he also discovers something euphoric and completely unexpected inside. As is suggested by the art and poetry here, it is believed that when we risk to feel those feelings we don't want to feel, and look inside, we can also discover the inner wonder and magic of who we are. The pain that we carry doesn't dissolve us. We are more than we imagined. The mythical and deeper message of The Little Bucket, not only for children, but for adults, connects us to that mysterious place inside, where we feel really alive and which nobody but we and the Bucket know about. It's the secret we've discovered, and it is ourselves. Conversely, children and adults know what it's like to give and give and feel like they're running out. Water into buckets with holes in the bottom. Maybe we have a hole in our bottom? How did it get there? We have to look inside to find out. But be ready, you might discover something else that you weren't expecting.

Often at the beginning when feeling our feelings it seems like a dance. We're not sure how to get in the dance. The feelings that are asking us to dance are new. The dancing couple on page 35 represents the dance of new feelings. The dance to feeling our feelings often gets delayed, even through adulthood, because sometimes it's hard, painful work. It's this kind of unresolved personal pain that leads to deep marital problems, blaming others for our problems and over-medicating our stress. We hide from the dancing partner on the inside. But the feelings beckon us, like a hand pulling us onto the dance floor, to dance anyway. They don't go away. The Little Bucket tries to hide too. But he teaches us not to. He dances by looking within. We can learn to embrace our joy, by dancing with our sadness. It's kind of strange how it happens. Many, many times sadness masks itself as emptiness. If you feel empty, then you can put the blame on your unfelt sadness, and not on others. We have to learn to navigate these waters within and not expect others to fill our bucket. Many empty people reveal an excess of sadness. Children sometimes don't know what to do with painful feelings, like sadness, fear and anger so they hide from them and pretend they are not there especially if there are no adults present who support them and model this healthy approach to feelings. This is unfortunate because feelings like this turn into depression and chronic loneliness. Eventually, without intervention, these unacknowledged feelings turn good kids into bullies and victims. Bullies and victims are buckets with holes. They have the same problem. The bully crosses everyone's boundaries and the victim doesn't have the confidence to set boundaries. Like two sides of one coin. Bullies look for victims to fill them up! And many times, victims end up being pleasers and followers who go along with bullies out of their hole-like fear. So the best way to help the bully and victim is to help them learn to feel the dance within themselves, and stop the dance with each other. And the best way to get the dance underway, is through a mythical story, through the music of a metaphor like The Little Bucket. It will be like hearing the music of our ancestors. I am convinced that this metaphor can break through and into our desperate situation today. It will be something like a sound that catches us. Like a beautiful song that we once knew. We are in urgent need of a story that can help us. When we read it and hear it, the music of life, and dance of the joy of life, can return. Kids can discover something within that they didn't know was there because to this point it hasn't made a sound. Our imaginations will dance. We'll dance in our conversations with kids. Children will dance with us.

Each time you invite The Little Bucket into your hearing, you invite a new conversation and new wisdom and depth to be discovered. Many inspired conversations and questions will come up. I have had many of them already! On the next page, there is a series of Little Bucket questions for adults to engage children and listen to them. Remember empathy and the fluid from the stars as you do. In this time, you will come up with your own questions too. These conversations will deepen you and your understanding and will give your children the feeling that you really do care about what is happening with them *on the inside*. They will come out of hiding. They will look lighter and brighter and you may notice something different happening. These little buckets will feel empathy from your effort. And they just may learn to splash each other too. It will take some practice. We must make a start. The time is now. I believe The Little Bucket can help us.

May the bucket you are be full! Happy splashing!

Jeffrey Bates

May 2014

In discussing this book, it would be a good idea to check in with the children about their feelings. You might ask how they feel after hearing it. Some might say "sad" and some might say "happy." Some additional discussion points.

1. Have you ever felt full like The Little Bucket? Have you ever felt you could splish and splash and that you would never run out? Tell about a time when it was like this for you.

2. Why do you think The Little Bucket started to leak?

3. Why do you think that nothing worked at first to get The Little Bucket filled back up even though he was trying so hard?

4. Have you ever felt that people were trying to make you happy and that nothing worked? What is going on there?

5. Have you ever tried to make someone else happy and it didn't work? How did you feel?

6. What are some things or who are some people who really make you feel happy and keep your bucket full? Can you name some people in your life who are full buckets? How can you tell?

7. What does it feel like to be made fun of by someone? What does it feel like to be ignored by someone? What do you feel like doing when this happens to you?

8. In the story of The Little Bucket, who do you think *the young boy in the yellow shirt* is? Did you even notice him? Do you think he is important?

9. What does *the hound* have to do with anything? Is the hound important?

10. When the Little Bucket was trying to hide from *the feeling inside*, did you know what he was doing? Have you ever tried to hide from your feelings? Talk about that.

11. Who can really fill up our bucket? Who is supposed to fill up our bucket? How do you know?

12. The Little Bucket discovers the hole AND the universe in his bucket. What could this mean?

13. When the *unhappy* bucket, from the beginning of the story, shows back up toward the end, how did that make you feel? Has anything like this ever happened to you? Tell about a time.

14. Why does the book end with "The End ~ And the Beginning?" What does the author want us to realize?

For more information and/or to order products and promotional materials for your school or event visit *The Little Bucket* at http://thelittlebucket.com. See web site to request author visit. Book reading, signing, discussion time for your event are available. Inquiries for such should be sent to The Little Bucket himself. Email the bucket: bucket@thelittlebucket.com.

This book was created using original drawings and poetry. Photoshop brushes included are from http://starwalt.com (Starfields) and Charfades ultimate grass brush set which can be found @http://charfade.devianart.com. Both were used with permission.

Please LIKE The Little Bucket on Facebook and follow him on Twitter @thelittlebucket.

If you should be more interested in myth see any work by Joseph Campbell, including, but not limited to:
Joseph Campbell, <u>The Power of Myth</u>, Apostrophe S Productions, 1988. (Book, DVD and AUDIO CD) Paraphrased quote can be found here. The audio CD's are an excellent resource.
Joseph Campbell, <u>The Hero With A Thousand Faces</u>, Bollingen Foundation Inc., New York, 1949.

References and other interesting works:

Jacob Grimm, <u>Household Tales by Brothers Grimm</u>, A Public Domain Book, Kindle Edition. Original stories based on the 1884 translation "Household Tales" of Margaret Hunt.
Rollo May, <u>The Art of Counseling</u>, Abingdon Press, New York, 1939. (*Quote used is from page 92).
Michael Meade, <u>The World Behind The World</u>, Greenfire Press, Seattle, WA, 2008.
Robert Bly, <u>Iron John</u>, Addison-Wesley Publishing Company, Reading, MA, 1990. A book about men for men to discover a connection to the wild man archetype. This is a poetic and enchanting interpretation of this classic Grimm's Fairy tale.
Clarissa Pinkola Estes, <u>Women Who Run With The Wolves</u>, Ballantine Books, New York, 1992. This is a book for women to discover the "myths and stories of the wild woman archetype."
Carl G. Jung, <u>Man and His Symbols</u>, Dell Publishing/Random House, 1964.
Eric Fromm, <u>Escape From Freedom</u>, Avon Books, 1941.

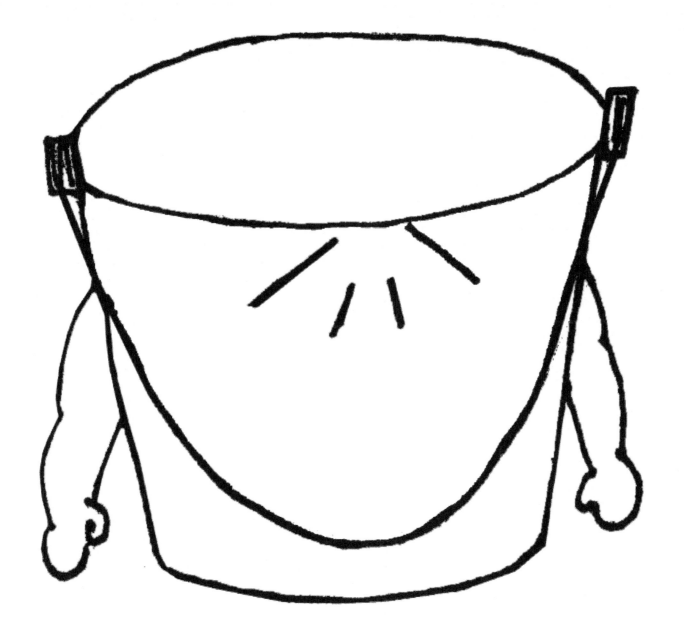

Hey, if you ever feel empty or afraid or lonely or angry, just think about me. I'll be right here.
Go ahead and color me too, and feel the colors as you do...you can do it!
Love, The Little Bucket

CPSIA information can be obtained at www.ICGtesting.com
Printed in the USA
BVOW07s1421281115

428522BV00014B/244/P